D0756657

Diamondz
Road Trip

by Christine Peymani

Bath · New York · Singapore · Hong Kong · Cologne · Delhi · Melbourne

First published by Parragon in 2007
Parragon
Queen Street House
4 Queen Street
Bath BA1 1HE, UK

ISBN 978-1-4054-9165-5

Printed in China

CHAPTER 1

"Welcome to America Rocks Fashion!" exclaimed Byron Powell.

Cloe, Jade, Sasha and Yasmin had first met the big-time reality TV producer when they formed their very own band, the Rock Angelz. Now, he was hosting a new reality show — starring them!

The girls watched the broadcast from inside their fashion big rig, which they'd be using for their cross-county fashion road trip. Emblazoned on one side was the logo of their very own Bratz Magazine. Next to them sat a bright pink big rig, which belonged to their rival magazine, Your Thing.

"I'm here in beautiful Stilesville to launch the season finale's adventure in fashion!" Byron continued.

©MGA

"Somewhere in the heartland of America, a teen designer waits to be discovered. This Wednesday morning, our two teams, rival fashion magazines Your Thing and Bratz, set out in their rollin' runways to find the hottest new designer out there!"

The crowd that had gathered for the live taping cheered wildly!

"They'll visit three small towns across the country, and each team will pick one girl from each town to continue on with them," Byron explained. "The teams have to get to New York by Saturday night, where the six contestants will model their own fashions in the America Rocks Fashion Show! The winner will get a contract with designer Mucci Fiari, plus a pair of diamond go-go boots — absolutely, positively priceless!"

Byron held up a gorgeous, sparkling pair of boots — definitely the glammest shoes ever!

"Now let's meet our teams," Byron said, heading for the trucks.

"That's our cue!" Jade exclaimed. She and

her best friends leapt up and hurried to the truck's back door, where a crew unfolded a catwalk for them to strut down. The girls worked the catwalk, smiling and waving to the cheering audience.

"Here comes our first team – Bratz Magazine!" Byron exclaimed. "Everyone knows the girls with a passion for fashion – Cloe, Yasmin, Sasha and Jade! And here's the competing team…"

On cue, a crew opened the back of the huge pink truck and folded out another catwalk. Burdine stepped onto it, decked out from head to toe in bright pink and cradling her snooty dog, Royale, who yapped fiercely at Byron.

Byron glared back and, sounding annoyed, said, "Your Thing Magazine, represented by Burdine Maxwell."

"That's me!" Burdine interrupted. "Founder, President, Editor-in-Chief and the reigning Queen of Fashion!"

She posed, waiting for the applause to

start, but was met with silence.

Suddenly the Tweevils, Burdine's obnoxious twin interns, burst onto the catwalk. Cloe, Yasmin, Sasha and Jade called them the 'Tweevils' because they were always so mean – they were like real-life evil twins!

"Don't forget us!" Kaycee cried.

"Yeah!" Kirstee exclaimed. "Without us, Your Thing would be no-thing."

"Get back in that truck, you ridiculous, pathetic interns," Burdine snarled.

Byron motioned for the cameraman to turn away from the Your Thing truck, but as Burdine continued yelling, the camera swung back over to capture the fight.

"Go, go, GO!" Burdine shouted as she struggled to herd the twins backstage.

"No fair," Kaycee whined.

"We wanna be on camera!" Kirstee complained. "Come on, let us say something!"

Burdine stepped in front of the twins,

trying to block them from the camera's view, flashing a huge, fake smile. Royale kept yapping and lunging towards Byron, who covered his ears, looking pained. But when he saw the camera on him again, he announced cheerfully, "We'll be right back to start our fashion road trip!"

"Three minutes for commercial, people!" shouted the assistant director. "Let's pack it up and get ready to move out!"

"Well, that was perfectly dreadful," Byron said in his proper British accent, all his on-air confidence disappearing.

"Nah, I thought it was slick," replied the cameraman. "You're the man, Mr Powell."

"Yes, yes," Byron grumbled.

The crew started packing up the catwalks as the girls loaded their suitcases into their truck.

"Put that one over there," Cloe directed as her friends tried to help her hoist another huge bag into the truck.

"Are you sure you need all of these, Angel?" Sasha asked.

'Angel' was Cloe's nickname because she was such a sweetie — and always looked totally heavenly. The girls had all packed tons of super-cool outfits, of course, but Cloe had managed to bring more suitcases than her three best friends combined!

"I'm just a little stressed out right now, ok?" said Cloe. "Let's just say this—" she gestured to her mountain of luggage, "—is my fashion security blanket."

"How can you be stressed when we're the stars of our own show all about fashion?" Jade asked.

©MGA

"It's just that I hate road trips," Cloe wailed. "They remind me of all those tedious, un-air-conditioned cross-country trips to Grandma's when I was a kid. We'd always be all crammed together in the family mini-van, and I totally had claustrophobia."

"Is that a fear of mini-vans?" Jade whispered to Yasmin.

"No – fear of small, confined spaces," Yasmin explained.

"Oh come on, Angel," Sasha said. "You know this is gonna be a blast!"

"I'm totally psyched," Jade added. "I've always wanted to scope out America, coast to coast!"

"It's not the fairyland you're imagining, Kool Kat," Cloe warned. Jade's friends called her 'Kool Kat' because she was always totally chilled out, and her fashion sense was the absolute coolest! "There's a lot of greasy food, wide open spaces and boring small towns out there – not good for someone with agoraphobia, like me!"

"That's fear of spiders, right?" Jade asked Yasmin.

"You're thinking of arachnophobia," Yasmin told her. "Agoraphobia is a fear of wide open spaces. I don't know what you call a fear of small towns, though." Turning to Cloe, she added, "Come on, Angel — small towns are quaint!"

"Quaint?" Cloe demanded. "Don't you know what happens on the open road? Don't you?!"

Byron approached and looked back and forth between the girls, trying to figure out what could have caused Cloe's outburst.

"Places, everyone!" called the assistant director.

"Ladies?" Byron interrupted. "It's time to get in your truck. On my signal, you'll start your engine and roll out!"

"Got it, Byron!" Sasha replied. "Angel, you're driving first."

Byron pulled Cloe aside and asked, "Pray tell — what does happen on the open road?"

"You know, alien encounters, that guy with the hook who tries to get in your car, the cute stray dog that turns out to be a rat, the headless horseman…" Her voice got higher and higher with each urban legend she named.

Sasha grabbed Cloe by the shoulders and shook her slightly to snap her out of her freak-out session.

"Get a-hold of yourself," she commanded.

Cloe was known for her tendency to be overly dramatic, but this was a bit much, even for her!

"Don't worry about her," Jade told Byron. "She's just talking nonsense."

But Byron didn't look worried — actually, he looked like he'd just been struck with a great idea.

"Alien encounters?" he said. "Sounds absolutely, positively exciting to me!"

"Thirty seconds — let's go!" called the assistant director.

The girls climbed into their truck with Cloe

in the driver's seat. Glancing back, the girls saw Kaycee behind the wheel of the Your Thing truck.

"Bon voyage!" exclaimed Byron. "I'll see you at the first town!"

Byron had a huge smile on his face as he bounded back to his place in front of the camera.

"A rustic road trip with no mobile phones, no GPS — just a map to guide their way," he said dramatically. "Thrilling!" Motioning to the trucks he announced, "Ladies, start your engines!"

The trucks revved up, their huge engines growling. Byron held up a green flag in front of the trucks and then whipped it down. The two trucks raced out of the car park — the great fashion hunt had officially begun!

In the Your Thing truck, Kaycee steered wildly, almost running Byron down.

"Wheeee!" she squealed. "We're off!"

Burdine clutched a squirming Royale to her chest as Kaycee's crazed driving knocked her from side to side.

"Watch out, you maniac!" Burdine screeched.

"You should let me drive!" Kirstee yelled from the back of the truck. "I've only failed two driving tests – she's failed four!"

Back in the Bratz truck, Cloe swerved to avoid the Your Thing truck.

"Hey!" she shouted at the other truck. "Watch where you're going!" She clutched her stomach dramatically and moaned, "Oooh, I'm already carsick!"

In the mall car park, Byron was wrapping up his broadcast.

"Catch up with us tomorrow as our two teams pick up their first teen fashion designer! Until then, this is Byron Powell, rocking America's fashion scene!"

The friends couldn't wait to get to the first stop on their fashion road show. "This is gonna be great!" Jade squealed.

"I'm totally pumped," Sasha agreed.

"What could be better than hittin' the road with my very best friends?" Yasmin added.

The girls all cheered, and even Cloe joined in, despite her anxiety.

Chapter 2

Hours into the drive, with no end in sight, the girls were starting to see why Cloe hated road trips. Yasmin and Sasha were fast asleep in the back, leaning on each other's shoulders, while Jade struggled to keep her eyes open in the front seat.

Sasha stirred and stretched, awaking from a long nap.

"Are we there yet?" she asked through a yawn.

"Not even close," Cloe replied grimly.

Yasmin woke up at the sound of their voices.

"Ouch," she moaned. "My legs are asleep."

Jade glanced back at her and asked, "What's that all over your shoulder?"

Yasmin looked down at the wet patch on her shirt and hit Sasha lightly on the arm.

"Bunny Boo! You drooled all over me!" she complained.

Sasha's love for urban music and street-inspired styles had earned her the nickname 'Bunny Boo'.

"Oh," Sasha murmured, still half-asleep. Then, noticing Yasmin's glare, she added, "Sorry!"

"Sooo…" Jade began, "tell me again why we couldn't get Byron to just fly us cross-country?"

"The things we do for Byron," Cloe sighed.

"Yeah, but think of all the cool experiences we've had since we met him," Sasha protested.

"True," Yasmin admitted. "But he has put us through a lot."

"But it's worth it," Sasha insisted. "Byron's totally my role model. I can only hope to achieve

14

my goals like he has. Just think of everything he's accomplished — I mean, he's been a TV show host and a secret government agent!"

"But I don't know why we always have to help him achieve his goals," Cloe complained.

"C'mon, Angel — think of what the publicity will do for our magazine!" Yasmin reminded her.

"Yeah, if we win," Cloe cried. "If Burdine's contestant wins, we'll look like total fools on live national TV! And then this heinous road trip will all have been for nothing."

"Where's your sense of adventure, people?" Sasha demanded. "Road trips are the best — you never know what's around the next corner."

Just then, Cloe noticed a creepy-looking hitchhiker standing on the side of the road. A bandana over his face covered most of what wasn't already hidden beneath a tattered hat. Cloe shuddered and turned away.

"Hey, I brought some of my organic tofu sprout rolls," Yasmin said. "Anybody want one?"

No one answered and Yasmin shrugged, popping a roll into her mouth.

"Mmmm," she said.

"Yo, Cloe?" Jade asked. "When can we break out those cookies you baked?"

Cloe stared out the window, totally distracted by the scary vision she'd just driven past.

"Uh, Cloe?" Yasmin called. "Are you asleep at the wheel, or what?"

Cloe snapped out of it. "Huh?" she asked. "Sorry Pretty Princess — what did you say?"

The girls all called Yasmin 'Pretty Princess' because of her totally regal, super-elegant style.

"Cookies!" Yasmin exclaimed. "We want your cookies!"

Cloe glanced at her watch, then replied, "Sorry — not till the next state border. We have to make our snacks last."

Her best friends all heaved huge sighs of disappointment.

"Hey, she can't stop us from going through her stuff," Jade pointed out. "She's driving!"

"Hmm. That's right," Sasha agreed. "Go for it, girls! Find those cookies!"

"Hey!" Cloe protested, turning her attention back to her friends. "Don't you dare!"

In the Your Thing truck, Kaycee's driving had gone from bad to worse. As she swerved wildly across several lanes of traffic, Burdine struggled to pull the girl out of the driver's seat.

"You're through, Kaycee!" Burdine cried. "I'm taking over!"

"I swear I'll do better!" Kaycee whimpered, fighting to keep control of the wheel. But Burdine was too strong for her — she grabbed the girl and shoved her into the passenger seat, where Kaycee landed on her sister with a thump. Burdine took the driver's seat.

"Hey, I called shotgun," Kirstee whined,

trying to wiggle out from under her twin. "Get off of me!"

"Kirstee, you know I can't sit in the back," Kaycee complained. "I get carsick!"

"Fine," Kirstee snapped, climbing into the back. "Whatever it takes to keep you from barfing!"

Burdine was struggling to regain control of the truck when suddenly the hitchhiker Cloe had seen appeared in the middle of the road.

"Out of my way, hick!" Burdine screamed.

The hitchhiker leapt out of the way at the last second and rolled behind a tumbleweed. "Ha!" Burdine crowed. "That's what you get for loitering in the road!"

"Yeah!" Kirstee chimed in. "Like, get a car, loser!"

"Loser, loser!" Kaycee chanted as they sped away.

"You know what we need?" Sasha asked her friends.

"A chauffeur? A four-star hotel? Not to be

on this dumb road trip in the first place?" Cloe suggested grumpily.

"No!" Sasha replied. "We need some music to get this party started! Come on, Cloe, turn on some tunes."

Grudgingly, Cloe reached over and flipped on the radio – and one of the girls' favourite songs blared out!

"See, Angel, that's gotta be a good sign, right?" Yasmin asked.

Cloe finally cracked a smile and joined in as

©MGA

her best friends sang along, groovin' to the music.

When the song ended, Cloe asked, "Hey, can someone check the map? I think we should've hit Route 66 by now."

"I'll be your designated navigator," Jade offered, spreading the map out on her lap. "Hmmm…" She traced their route with one long, perfectly manicured finger. "It looks like it's coming up soon…"

Just then, they flew past a Route 66 road sign. "Never mind!" Cloe exclaimed. "I found it!"

"Always glad to help," Jade said with a smile.

The girls kept jammin' and singing along to the radio as they drove down the open road, passing gorgeous mountains and rolling fields. Jade leaned her head out of the window, enjoying the breeze.

"Can you imagine living out here?" Yasmin asked dreamily.

"Absolutely not," Jade replied, pulling her head back inside the truck. "I mean, I haven't seen a mall in hours!"

"That would be a drawback," Yasmin admitted.

They whizzed past the Grand Canyon, the Hoover Dam – and the world's biggest ball of yarn.

"What is that?" Sasha demanded.

"It's a giant ball of yarn," Yasmin explained.

"But why?" Sasha asked.

"Because it's totally boring out here!" Jade replied. "Just like I thought! Just imagine – if we lived this far from a mall, we might be making our very own giant yarn balls right now."

"Scary thought," Sasha said. She stared out the window at the endless cornfields and sighed. "Okay, now I miss the giant ball of yarn. I'm totally bored."

She whipped a mini manicure kit out of her bag and carefully gave herself a perfect

French manicure as Yasmin watched in amazement.

"How can you paint your nails so perfectly when we're bouncing around in this truck?" Yasmin asked as Sasha blew on her nails to dry them.

"Hey, is that a comment on my driving?" Cloe called back from the front seat. She flinched as an insect hit the windscreen and splattered. Cloe flipped on the windscreen wipers, totally grossed out.

"Of course not, Angel," Yasmin replied soothingly. "You're doing an awesome job." Turning to Sasha, she added, "But seriously, that's amazing!"

"Why thank you," Sasha said modestly, dangling her hand out the window to speed up the drying process. She spotted some cows and waved to them cheerfully. Maybe this road-trip thing wasn't so bad after all.

Chapter 3

But as they continued down the highway, the road grew totally desolate. There was nothing but flat road in front of them and empty fields in every direction. The girls broke out the bag of Cloe's cookies and munched on them happily — cookies were a great diversion!

They were all focused on their cookies when Cloe noticed that same creepy hitchhiker standing at the side of the road.

"Omigosh!" Cloe cried, so startled that she dropped her cookie. "Did you see that?"

Yasmin looked up, but the hitchhiker had already disappeared. "See what?" she asked.

"I just saw the same hitchhiker I saw hours ago," Cloe wailed.

"A hitchhiker?" Yasmin said. "How sad. Maybe we should pick him up."

"Are you out of your mind?" Cloe

screeched. "You can't pick up hitchhikers – they could be psychopathic maniacs. You never talk to strangers, you never take a ride from a stranger and you never ever EVER pick up a hitchhiker!"

"Yeah, Yasmin," Sasha agreed.

"Besides, did you see that hitchhiker?" Cloe demanded.

"I didn't see anyone," Jade replied.

"Neither did I," Yasmin chimed in.

"I'm telling you, it was the same guy I saw before," Cloe insisted.

Yasmin, Sasha and Jade exchanged concerned looks behind Cloe's back.

"I think we need a rest stop," Sasha said. "I know too much driving always makes me a little crazy."

"I don't need a rest stop!" Cloe exclaimed. "And I'm not crazy!"

24

"No one's saying you're crazy, Angel," Sasha continued soothingly.

"I know what I saw!" Cloe cried. "It's just like that story about the ghost hitchhiker who ends up on the back seat. You see him in the rear-view mirror and then –"

"Okay, okay," Jade interrupted. "It's gonna be okay, Cloe. Maybe you're just suffering from a little cabin fever."

"I do not have cabin fever!" Cloe protested.

"Well, maybe I do," Yasmin replied. "Come on – let's pull over at the next stop."

"I'm going to the toilet," Cloe grumbled once they had parked. "I hope they have toilet paper."

She headed towards a drab-looking cinderblock building marked 'Toilets'. But as she turned the corner, she was horrified to see the hitchhiker leaning against the building.

"Eeek!" Cloe screamed, backing away slowly and looking around desperately for her friends. She spotted them hanging out by the truck and broke into a run to join them.

"Guys! Guys!" she shouted.

Yasmin turned. "What is it, Angel?" she asked.

"I saw him...over there...by the toilets," Cloe gasped.

"Who?" Sasha asked.

"The hitchhiker!" Cloe cried.

"Let's go take a look!" Sasha said.

Cloe led her friends around the side of the building to the spot where the hitchhiker had been lurking moments before. But there was no one there.

"It's really hot out, Cloe," Jade said.

The girls headed for the truck, shaking their heads.

"No, Jade, you don't understand," Cloe protested. "He was there!"

"Sure, we believe you," Yasmin agreed, trying to calm Cloe down.

"It was him," Cloe insisted. "Old hat, bandana, boots, overcoat."

"An overcoat? In this heat?" Jade asked.

Yasmin, Jade and Sasha all shook their heads. "Nuh-uh," they said in unison. They climbed back into the truck as Cloe fumed. She couldn't believe her best friends didn't believe her!

In the Your Thing truck, Burdine sat in the driver's seat, clenching the wheel and glaring at the road ahead. Her dog, Royale, was strapped into the seat next to her, while the Tweevils sat in the back, loudly singing an off-key round.

"Row, row, row your boat, gently down the stream. Merrily, merrily, merrily, merrily, life is but a dream!" they shrieked.

Burdine glanced at the twins in the rear-view mirror, just missing the hitchhiker standing alongside the road.

"Yoo-hoo! Tweedle-dumb and Tweedledumber!" she called. "Can it, will you? You're making my life a nightmare!"

The girls had stopped for the night at a roadside motel. Jade, Sasha and Yasmin were on their way back to their room from the hot tub, wrapped in bathrobes and carrying towels. They spotted Cloe coming towards them, bathrobe and towel in hand and an angry look on her face.

"Hey Angel," Jade greeted her. "You should've come with us. The hot tub was great."

"Yes, I think I'll go and enjoy it now," Cloe snapped.

"Cloe, you aren't still mad at us, are you?" Sasha asked, surprised.

"No. Not mad," Cloe replied, her tone dripping sarcasm. "Unless you mean mad as in crazy. Bats. Nuts. Loony. OFF HER ROCKER!"

She stalked off towards the hot tub.

"Cloe!" Jade called after her. She started

to follow her friend, but Sasha stopped her.

"Wait, Jade," Sasha said. "Maybe she just needs a little alone time."

But at the entrance to the hot tub, Cloe was having second thoughts about that. "Maybe my friends are right," she mused. "Maybe I'm just imagining things."

Just then she looked up and saw the hitchhiker soaking in the hot tub — hat, bandana, overcoat and all! She screamed as loud as she could, and ran.

Chapter 4

The next morning, Cloe drove down the highway at a manic speed, her eyes darting nervously from side to side.

"Are you sure you don't need a break, Cloe?" Jade asked tentatively.

"Quite sure," Cloe replied sharply.

"You've been driving all day," Yasmin insisted. "Let one of us take over."

"I just want to get there," Cloe snapped.

"Okay, okay," Sasha said, trying to calm her friend down.

Suddenly, Cloe's eyes widened in terror — there, at the side of the road, stood the hitchhiker, his thumb jutting out insistently towards the truck. Frightened, Cloe swerved, making her friends scream as they were jerked to the side.

"Whoa," Sasha said. "What happened?"

"Nothing," Cloe replied firmly. She pressed her foot on the gas, taking the truck as fast as it could go.

"Angel, slow down!" Jade pleaded. The Bratz truck flew past the Your Thing truck and a sign reading 'Rockwater Springs'.

"We're here!" Cloe announced in a manically chipper voice.

Cloe screeched to a halt and climbed out of the truck while Sasha, Yasmin and Jade exchanged panicked looks.

"What's with our girl?" Sasha whispered to Yasmin and Jade.

"She's been acting really weird ever since last night..." Jade mused.

"Yeah, when she came back from the hot tub," Yasmin agreed.

"No more driving for her," Sasha decided, following Cloe out of the truck.

The girls spent the day searching the first town on their list, Rockwater Springs, for their first contestant. That night, a crowd of cheering teenage girls gathered around the Bratz and Your Thing trucks for the live broadcast. Yasmin, Sasha, Jade and Cloe posed at the end of their catwalk, while Burdine stood at the end of hers. Meanwhile, the Tweevils were stuck in the audience.

"Like, I can't believe she won't even let us be on TV with her," Kaycee complained.

©MGA

"Yea-ah," Kirstee whined. "We should totally be in the fashion show. I'm mean, we're doing all the work and some no-talent girl is going to get all the credit."

On camera, Byron spoke into his hip-looking microphone headset. "And now, the moment we've all been waiting for!" He turned to the girls.

"Who will be our first contestant from Bratz Magazine?" he asked.

Yasmin stepped forward and announced, "Our pick from Rockwater Springs is…Mandy Pickett!"

A piercing shriek of excitement rang out from the crowd. Mandy, a cute girl in a cowboy hat and fringed top, ran to the front of the audience as the crowd cheered her on. The girls reached down to help her onto the catwalk, and then gave her a big, welcoming group hug.

"Congratulations, Mandy Pickett!" Byron exclaimed.

Through tears of joy, Mandy cried, "I'm so happy!" in her sweet Southern accent. She started strutting up and down the Bratz catwalk, looking like a professional model with a sweet, shy glow. In the audience, the Tweevils rolled their eyes.

"Whatever," Kaycee said.

"Mandy is wearing a darling outfit she designed in her high school enrichment class," Byron read from his notecard. "It's absolutely, positively fabulous! Mandy also loves horses, children and most of all, she wants to help others. Let's give it up for our first contestant, Mandy!"

Burdine glared at Mandy from the Your Thing catwalk. "Look at the trash they picked out," she muttered. "She doesn't stand a chance!"

"And now for Your Thing's first contestant," Byron continued. "Your Thing? Who is your lucky…" he paused, unable to bring himself to call the Your Thing contestant 'lucky'. "Well, who have you selected from

Rockwater Springs?"

"Christy Baker!" Burdine declared

Another scream rang out from the audience and Christy rushed forward. But this time, no one from town cheered her on. The audience just looked at each other, puzzled at the choice.

Only Christy's dad seemed to share her excitement. "Way to go, Buttercup," he called out. "Daddy looooves you!"

Reaching the front of the audience, Christy declared in a fake French accent, "Ooh la la! This is quel magnifique!" She looked exactly like the Tweevils, but with even more pink and bows piled onto her outfit.

The Tweevils stared at her in disgust.

"What a slob," Kirstee snarled. "I wouldn't be caught dead wearing something like that."

"She has, like, no style at all," Kaycee agreed.

Christy scurried onto the Your Thing catwalk, gave Burdine an air kiss and went right into strutting her stuff. She made totally obnoxious faces and struck horrible-looking poses — she was an absolute disaster, but Burdine looked on with obvious pride.

Byron read Christy's bio on-air, sounding utterly annoyed.

"Christy Baker knew from the moment she was born that she was going to take over the fashion world with her totally 'chic' designs. Pink is her signature colour and she can't wait to enlighten the world with her fashion point of view."

"She's got to be kidding," Sasha said.

"It's another Tweevil," Cloe agreed.

"Now they're Threevils!" Yasmin declared, shaking her head.

After Christy finally got off the stage, Byron wrapped up the show, and soon the girls hit the road again. They drove along an empty desert highway with Jade at the wheel and Mandy in the passenger seat beside her.

"I'm so excited ya'll picked me!" Mandy

squealed. "It's a dream come true. Thank you, thank you, thank you!"

"You can stop thanking us, Mandy," Yasmin said. "You deserve it. Your fashions are really cool."

"Yeah, you have a great sense of style," Jade agreed. Just then, she spotted a detour sign ahead. "Uh-oh, detour." She started following the signs, which were aimed totally out of their way.

"Oh no," Sasha complained. "I'm starving."

Cloe spotted a neon sign reading 'Sidewinder Café' just off the road.

"There's a café," she said. "Let's stop."

"Sounds good to me!" Sasha replied.

The girls pulled into the Sidewinder Café's car park and climbed out. As they neared the restaurant's entrance, Burdine's truck roared up and parked beside them.

"Oh no!" Jade whispered. "It's Burdine!"

"And the Threevils!" Yasmin added.

"Who are the Threevils?" Mandy asked.

"Oh…" Yasmin replied. "It's just that Burdine's interns and her first contestant kind of look like triplets."

"Oh, y'all mean Christy?" Mandy said.

"Yeah, you must go to school with her, huh?" Jade asked.

"Well, actually, no," Mandy replied. "She goes to a boarding school in Switzerland. But I'm sure she's a very nice girl."

"That's very…nice of you," Cloe said, surprised.

"Well, I only like to say nice things about other folks," Mandy explained.

"Wow, that's totally admirable," Sasha replied.

"C'mon y'all, let's grab some grub," said Mandy, motioning the girls towards the restaurant.

The girls settled into a booth in the diner. While their first contestant went to wash her hands, Yasmin said, "We should really try to be more like Mandy – I mean, what a positive attitude!"

"You're right, Pretty Princess," Jade agreed. "We shouldn't say so many bad things about the Tweevils and Burdine."

Mandy returned to their table and, just then, Burdine entered with Royale in her arms. Kirstee, Kaycee and Christy followed her in. Burdine stared at the girls and their contestant, smirking.

"You Bratz don't stand a chance," Burdine declared. "You couldn't pick a winner in a contest of one."

"That's not very nice!" Mandy gasped.

"Can it, cowgirl," Burdine snapped.

"Where's the square dance?" Kirstee asked Mandy. Kaycee gave her a high five.

"Yeah, like, when's the hayride?" Kaycee asked. "Wouldn't want to miss it."

Mandy looked horrified as Burdine, Royale and the Threevils strutted through the restaurant and perched themselves on stools at the counter.

"Just look at this shack," Burdine complained, looking around the diner disdainfully. "Let's hope they have something edible."

Mandy leaned across the table towards the four friends and whispered, "My goodness. They're…"

"Go ahead," Cloe encouraged her.

"Say it," Yasmin added.

"…different," Mandy finished. The others stared at Mandy, amazed at her charitable nature.

Suddenly Dot, a barrel-shaped waitress with hairy legs and muscular arms, came running out of the kitchen carrying a steaming pot of coffee.

She stomped up to Burdine and asked, "What'll it be, Pinky?"

"Do you have a green salad?" Burdine asked.

Dot snorted. "Green? Here? Ha! When you dream, you dream big, dontcha toots?"

"Excuse me, Madame?" Christy asked in her snooty accent. "Where might I find your powder room?"

"My what?" Dot asked, confused.

Christy leaned towards Dot conspiratorially and whispered, "Your ladies' room."

"Ah! The outhouse? It's out back," Dot announced loudly, pointing the way.

Christy shuddered and, looking defeated, trudged out of the diner and around towards the back.

"Excuse me y'all?" Mandy said. "I think I'm gonna go powder my nose."

Mandy slipped out the door after Christy, and then the Tweevils followed them both into the darkness.

Chapter 5

Mandy still hadn't returned when Dot brought out the girls' order. Behind them, Burdine and Royale sat at the counter, waiting for the Threevils to reappear.

"How's it goin', ladies?" Dot asked them after she set down their food.

"Oh, fine," Jade replied.

"Where y'all headed?" Dot asked.

"New York City!" Cloe, Jade, Sasha and Yasmin all exclaimed together.

"Are you girls out there on the road all alone?" Dot asked.

"Yes, ma'am," Jade told her.

"Well, whatever you do, don't pick up any strangers," Dot warned.

Cloe looked at their waitress with interest.

"You see, there's an old legend in these

parts," Dot explained. "Maybe it's not a legend...maybe it's true."

"Wha-what is it?" Yasmin asked, frightened.

"It's about an old cowboy named Foul-mouthed Foley," Dot began. "He mouthed off too many times and ended up in a showdown. Caught a bullet right in the kisser — lost his jaw."

"You mean he doesn't have a mouth?" Cloe cried.

"No nose neither," Dot added.

©MGA

43

"Yuck!" Yasmin exclaimed.

"Now his ghost roams these parts, trying to catch a ride outta here," Dot continued. "You haven't seen him, have you?" She looked directly at Cloe, who was shaking with fear. "Cos once ya do…" the girls stared at Dot, mesmerized, "…why, he'll haunt you forever!"

Dot smacked her big, meaty hand down on the table, making all four girls jump.

In the meantime, the Tweevils were sneaking around the side of the diner.

"Like, I only see a phone booth," Kaycee said.

"Shhh, you bubble brain, that's the outhouse," Kirstee told her twin. "She's in there. This is our chance to get rid of her."

"Get rid of her?" Kaycee asked.

"Yeah," Kirstee explained. "Then Burdine will have to put us in the show."

"Hey! Good idea!" Kaycee said excitedly. "But how do we do it?"

"You'll see," Kirstee replied.

The twins tiptoed over to the outhouse. Kirstee found an axe lodged in a nearby tree stump and grabbed it. She winked at her sister and then shoved it through the handle of the outhouse, making it impossible to open.

Back in the diner, the friends sat in stunned silence at their table, their food forgotten.

"Could it be true?" Yasmin wondered.

"No way," Sasha said firmly. "It's just a tall story."

"Hey, Mandy's been gone a long time," Jade pointed out. "We'd better go find her — before the hitchhiker does."

The girls looked spooked as they headed outside to search for their contestant. They called Mandy's name, but couldn't find her. They were about to give up and head back inside when they heard an eerie, muffled voice in the distance.

"Help!" it wailed.

45

"Okay, you guys," Yasmin said, grabbing her friends' hands. "What was that?"

"Omigosh, I think he's got Mandy," Cloe cried.

Behind them, a dark shape loomed, its tattered hat outlined against the moon.

"Aaaaaahhhhh!" the girls screamed.

Then the figure stepped forward and the girls saw that it was only Mandy in her trademark cowboy hat. They slumped against each other in relief.

"Mandy, don't do that!" Cloe exclaimed.

"What, y'all?" Mandy asked, looking puzzled. "I was just using the lavatory."

"But if the hitchhiker didn't get you," Yasmin wondered, "then who was that calling for help?"

Inside, Burdine sat alone at the counter, glaring at the French fries scattered on her plate. Kirstee and Kaycee burst in, giggling.

"Where have you been?" Burdine demanded. "You haven't even ordered!"

"Oh, we're not hungry," Kaycee said.

"Where's Kirst—Kay—Kiskie—Christy?" Burdine asked.

"Oh, she wanted us to tell you," Kirstee said casually. "She got homesick and took a cab home."

Burdine leapt off her stool. "What?!" she shouted.

Outside, Dot headed for the outhouse and discovered that the door was jammed shut with the axe handle. From inside the outhouse, Christy whimpered feebly.

Dot removed the axe and Christy burst out. When she saw Dot looming over her with the axe raised above her head, she screamed and ran away as fast as she could.

"Um, why are the lights out?" Sasha asked as she and her friends headed back to the diner.

"They couldn't have closed," Yasmin said. "We haven't even paid yet."

Jade tried the door, and it slowly creaked

47

open to reveal the whole diner covered in spiders' webs and dust, as though it had been abandoned for years.

"Ahhhhhhhhh!!" Cloe, Jade, Sasha, Yasmin and Mandy shrieked.

"Run!" Jade shouted. The girls backed away from the door and ran for the truck.

"Let's get out of here!" Cloe cried.

The girls piled into the truck and Jade started the engine. "Should we warn Burdine?" she asked.

"Just drive!" Cloe shouted.

Jade shot out of the car park, tyres squealing. Behind them, Kirstee, Kaycee and Burdine headed for their truck.

"Really, she went home," Kaycee insisted.

"Nonsense," Burdine snapped.

The hitchhiker appeared in front of them, looking menacing. Burdine and the Tweevils strolled right past him, unfazed. Kirstee paused to assess the hitchhiker's outfit and asked, "What is with the hat fashion

48

statement everyone's into out here?"

Burdine was unlocking the truck when Christy ran towards them, looking frantic, her hair and pink outfit dishevelled.

"There you are, Kayce–Kirst–Kris–Krispie," Burdine said. "I knew you didn't go home."

"Quel terrible!" Christy sobbed. "I couldn't get out of that outhouse!"

"Please, I don't need to hear the details," Burdine said.

"Then that waitress tried to kill me with an axe!" Christy continued.

"Well, she tried to kill me with French fries," Burdine said, unimpressed. "Now get in the truck."

As Jade drove down the dark, winding road, Sasha said, "We're so sorry we didn't believe you, Cloe."

"Guys, this is just like every story I've ever heard about creepy trips on the open road — and it's all coming true," Cloe replied frantically. "I want to go home."

"But we're supposed to be in Mount Middleton in an hour," Yasmin protested.

Mandy started crying and Sasha put her arm around the girl to comfort her. "Don't be afraid," Sasha said.

"It's just…all my dreams," Mandy said, wiping away her tears. "Y'all aren't really going to quit, are ya?"

"Omigosh, of course not!" Cloe said. "I'm so sorry, Mandy. I got so wrapped up in my own fears that I wasn't even thinking of anyone else. But we'll get you to New York and you'll have a totally fabulous fashion debut!"

Mandy cheered up right away.

"Thanks, gals," she said, her eyes gleaming.

©MGA

Chapter 6

Burdine drove behind the Bratz Magazine truck with Royale and Christy in the front seat beside her.

"Are you sure you don't want us to model your fashions for you?" Kaycee asked Christy. "I mean, you don't really want to be on TV, do you?"

"Yeah! I mean, aren't you embarrassed?" Kirstee added.

"Zut, alors!" Christy exclaimed. "Embarrassed by what?"

"Well, your looks," Kaycee said.

"And your outfit," Kirstee added. "Our fashions would be, like, so much better."

Suddenly, Christy whirled on them, her real Southern accent coming out.

"My looks? What about y'all's looks? And your clothes? Y'all dress like a pair of rodeo clowns. Just look at ya!"

"Oh no!" Kaycee cried.

The Tweevils launched themselves over the seat at Christy, clawing and shrieking and snarling.

"Kriskie—Cutesie—Katie—Kooky—whatever your names are!" Burdine shouted, completely losing her cool. "Cut it out, you horrible twits! Back in your seats, right now!"

Suddenly a loud bang echoed through the cab and the truck swerved out of control.

"Ahhhhh!" screamed Burdine. The Your Thing truck flew off the road and into a field.

Moments later, Burdine stumbled out of the truck, followed by the battle-worn Threevils. Burdine examined the tyre.

"Oh," she said wearily. "We've got a flat." She turned to the Tweevils and commanded, "Change it. Chop chop!"

"I don't know how to change a tyre!" Kaycee protested.

"Huh," Christy snorted in her Southern

accent. "Any fool can change a tyre."

"Ooh, that's it!" Kaycee shrieked, launching herself at Christy. Kirstee joined in, but Burdine stepped between them, holding all three girls back.

"Kirsk–Kisk–Kootie–Cookie – stop it!" she shouted.

The girls stopped struggling, but kept glowering at each other.

"If it's so easy, you change the tyre," Burdine ordered Christy.

"Do I look like one of my Daddy's ranch hands to you?" Christy demanded. "I don't change tyres. I just know it's a cinch, that's all."

"But this is an emergency – and you work for me now, Krispie," Burdine declared.

"I don't work for you, Granny," Christy snapped.

Burdine sputtered, her face turning an angry red.

"You want to be in this contest?" she

shouted. "Then change that tyre."

Christy immediately whipped out her mobile phone and speed-dialled her father.

"Hey! Like, no fair," Kirstee complained. "Mobile phones are so against the rules. She'll get us disqualified."

Ignoring her, Christy said into her phone, "Daddy? It's Princess. Come and git me."

"You can't quit now!" Burdine yelled.

But Christy turned her back on Burdine and the Tweevils, strode to the side of the highway and sat down to wait for her daddy to come and rescue her.

"I told you – you should've just picked us as your hot teen designers," Kirstee told Burdine, before stalking back to the truck with Kaycee.

Burdine sank to the ground, holding her head in her hands despairingly.

Eventually a huge car with longhorns mounted on its hood pulled up beside Christy.

"Hop in, Princess," her daddy called.

Christy slid gracefully into the seat beside him.

"Your mama's got a hot bath and some of her sweet po-tater pie waitin' fer ya back at the ranch," he said.

"Avec whipped cream?" Christy asked hopefully.

"Well of course avec whipped cream, my lil' buttercup!" Christy's dad replied as he peeled out, leaving Burdine behind in a cloud of dust.

"I want my daddy," Burdine whimpered.

"And here comes the second Bratz contestant, Tiffany!" Byron announced that night, broadcasting live from the town of Mount Middleton.

Tiffany hit the catwalk, showing off her ultra-cool, high-style fashions as the Bratz team looked on with pride.

"Isn't she fabulous?" Byron asked the camera. "And can you tell Tiffany's not a stranger to performing? She gives amateur magic shows at the local nursing home, where her speciality is sleight-of-hand."

In the audience, Mandy looked totally glum.

"Normally we would be introducing another contestant to you tonight," Byron continued. "But unfortunately the competition, Your Thing Magazine, hasn't shown up."

"Can you believe Burdine didn't show?" Cloe asked as she and her friends headed back to the truck.

"Maybe we scared her off!" Jade suggested.

She stuck Tiffany's suitcase in the truck while the new girl climbed into the back seat, a mini rucksack on her shoulder.

Sasha hopped out of the truck, looking frantic. "Girls, I can't find the keys!" she exclaimed. "Did I give them to one of you?"

Her friends all searched their stuff, but couldn't find the keys anywhere.

Byron strolled over and asked, "How's it going, ladies?"

"I don't have the keys," Cloe told Sasha, brushing past the show's host. "But — omigosh, my wallet's missing, too!"

"My money's gone, and so is my camera," Yasmin added, coming out of the truck. "And my shampoo!"

"Oh no," Jade cried. "My wallet's gone — and my kiwi-lime conditioner. How weird."

Tiffany stood by, looking concerned, while Mandy pawed through her bag.

"Oh no, y'all!" Mandy exclaimed. "Someone took my wallet too — and my hand lotion!" Mandy burst into tears. "My Grandma gave me that wallet for good luck."

"This is terrible!" Tiffany said. "You poor things."

She started to hug Mandy, but as she did, her rucksack shifted and something began to drip out of the bottom.

"Tiffany, I believe your rucksack's leaking," Byron told her.

"Uh-oh," Tiffany said. She took off her rucksack and started to unzip it.

"That's funny," Jade said. "I can smell my conditioner."

Tiffany peered into her rucksack. "Huh?" she asked, confused.

Everyone watched as Tiffany pulled a bottle of conditioner out of her rucksack. The lid had come unscrewed and the conditioner ran down the side of the bottle in a big, blobby mess.

"Wow, you use the same conditioner as me," Jade said.

"Wait, is that my wallet?" Cloe asked, spotting it inside Tiffany's rucksack.

Tiffany pulled a wallet covered in conditioner goo out of her bag. "What's this doing in here?" she wondered.

"Indeed," Byron said.

Tiffany removed another wallet and a bottle of hand lotion. "That's the wallet my Grandma gave me!" Mandy cried.

"Wait a second," Tiffany protested. "I don't understand!"

"Oh, but I understand perfectly," Byron said. "An amateur magician specializing in sleight-of-hand? I guess you've been putting your skills to work."

"What do you mean?" Tiffany asked.

"Ladies, she's a pickpocket!" Byron announced.

"No!" Tiffany protested. "I didn't...I wouldn't..."

Byron motioned a policeman over and the officer led Tiffany away as tears streamed down her face. The girls looked shocked, but Mandy looked strangely smug.

"I can't believe it," Jade said.

Her best friends shook their heads sadly.

"She seemed so cool," Yasmin agreed.

Byron darted back in front of the camera.

"And there we are," he announced. "Bratz Magazine has lost its second contestant and Your Thing didn't even arrive to collect theirs. Looks like things are getting pretty interesting. Tune in tomorrow to see what happens next on America Rocks Fashion!"

Chapter 7

Byron's crew was packing up their equipment when the Your Thing truck roared up. The puny wheel the Tweevils had used to replace their flat tyre thunked along beneath the big rig, making the truck wobble dangerously.

"A bit late, wouldn't you say, Miss Maxwell?" Byron asked.

"Someone put nails in our tyre!" Burdine wailed. "We were sabotaged!" She pointed at the girls accusingly. "It's those Bratz, I know it!"

"We didn't touch her truck!" Sasha protested.

"What paranoia!" Byron scolded Burdine. "Sounds like an ordinary road trip mishap to me. However, rules are rules and you've missed town number two, along with your chance at a second contestant."

While everyone was distracted by the new

arrivals, Mandy slipped away, sliding under the Your Thing truck without anyone noticing.

"What?" Burdine cried. "That's outrageous! I need my second girl. That Kirst–Kisk–Krisco–Christy person turned out to be a complete flake. She just walked out on us for no reason!"

"You don't say," Byron replied.

"Start those cameras up," Burdine demanded. "I'm ready to roll!"

"Then you can roll right out of here and on to town number three," Byron told her calmly. "And this time, try to be on time."

"Do as I say!" Burdine commanded. "Turn on that camera!"

"Temper, temper, Miss Maxwell," Byron replied.

Burdine glared at him, then turned on her heel and stalked back to the truck. She climbed in, slammed the door behind her and then leaned out the window to shout, "You'll be sorry, Bratz!"

Burdine threw the truck into reverse and peeled out, tyres screeching. Mandy reappeared beside the girls and watched the Your Thing truck go.

"Too bad that wasn't on camera," Byron said. "That woman is absolutely, positively impossible – but that was good TV."

Burdine drove at a manic pace to reach the next town ahead of the Bratz team. As she neared the town, she spotted a crossroads with signs pointing to different nearby small towns and swerved off the road.

"What are you doing?" Kaycee asked.

"You'll see," Burdine replied.

Soon she was crouching beside the road sign with Kaycee standing on her back and Kirstee balancing on her sister's shoulders. Kirstee banged on the sign pointing to Plainsville with a hammer, knocking it off the signpost. Then she banged on the sign for Dayton Place until it bent to point down a different road.

"Hurry up!" Burdine screeched. "My back is breaking."

Just then, Burdine felt something wet running down her leg.

"What in the name of pink is that?" she demanded.

Craning her neck, she saw that Royale had lifted his leg to wee on her.

"Nooooo!!" Burdine wailed as the Tweevils stifled their giggles.

The girls and Mandy sailed down the highway, singing along to the radio with Yasmin at the wheel. When Yasmin spotted the dented Dayton Place sign, she slowed down, signalled and turned right onto a path that led directly through the cornfields.

"Wow," Yasmin said as cornstalks whipped past the truck's windows. "This is real farmland."

"I hate cornfields," Cloe moaned.

"Why?" Mandy asked her.

"Cos, you know, aliens like cornfields," Cloe explained. "They're, like, really drawn to them."

"Cloe, don't start," Yasmin pleaded. "Guys, I think we're lost. I haven't seen a road sign for miles."

"Try this turn up here," Sasha suggested, pointing.

Yasmin made the turn, but all that lay in front of them was dirt road, darkness and corn.

In the Your Thing truck, Burdine drove through the night, a triumphant grin plastered across her face.

"Those Bratz have a surprise coming to them!" she crowed. She waited for the Tweevils to respond, and then glanced in the rear-view mirror and saw that they were both sound asleep.

"Finally, some peace,"

she sighed. Through the windscreen, she saw a cow crossing the road.

"Move it, Bessie!" she shouted.

Burdine hit the brakes, but the pedal sank all the way to the floor without slowing down the truck.

"What the...?" Burdine cried as the truck continued speeding towards the cow. "In the name of all that is pink! The brakes don't work!"

At the last second, Burdine swerved to avoid the cow. The truck flew off the road, landed with a jolt, and hurtled across a field and into a smelly green pond. A herd of cows stared at the truck, chewing their grass and looking bored.

"Those rotten Bratz!" Burdine cried from inside the truck.

The next morning, the girls awoke in their truck in the middle of a cornfield. Jade and Yasmin emerged groggily from the truck.

"Poor Mandy," Yasmin whispered. "I'm sure this isn't exactly the glamorous adventure she dreamed of."

Jade stretched her arms above her head and replied, "At least she's sleeping. I don't think I slept a wink."

Cloe and Sasha got out of the truck, just in time to overhear Jade.

"How could you?" Cloe asked. "I mean, look where we are! There could be aliens all around us, closing in right now."

"C'mon, Angel," Sasha said. "Aliens?"

"Hey, she was right about the hitchhiker," Yasmin pointed out. She had hardly finished speaking when they all heard a weird shuffling noise in the corn.

"What was that?" Jade cried. The girls huddled close together, terrified.

"It's coming from over there," Cloe said, pointing further into the cornfield with a trembling hand. A loud snapping sound came from that direction, and Sasha moved tentatively towards it.

"What are you doing, Bunny Boo?" Jade asked.

"Don't leave us," Cloe pleaded. "It's too dangerous!"

"I'm not leaving you," Sasha replied. "You're coming with me – to investigate." The girls looked at Sasha fearfully, but when she boldly moved forward, they followed her.

"Are you crazy?" Cloe demanded. "Let's get back in the truck and get out of here."

"Where would we go?" Sasha asked sensibly. "We're lost. Maybe it's a friendly farmer."

When the sound of breaking cornstalks approached from behind as well, Cloe gripped her best friends' hands in terror. "They're surrounding us!" she whispered.

They heard a loud crash behind them and Sasha shouted, "Run!"

The girls pushed through the corn and burst from between the stalks into a clearing, where they came face-to-face with a tall, creepy figure, silhouetted by the sun.

"Ahhhhhhh!!" screamed the four girls.

They fell to their knees, shutting their eyes tightly and turning away from the horrible creature that loomed over them.

"Ahhhhh!" shrieked another girl's voice from nearby.

The girls assumed it was Mandy, but just then Mandy strolled up and calmly asked them, "What's going on?"

The girls opened their eyes, squinting in the bright early-morning sunlight, and saw that the creepy figure that had completely freaked them out was just a scarecrow dressed in a cool T-shirt and jeans.

A teenage girl with long, dark hair and glasses hiding her face peered out from behind the scarecrow, looking just as scared as they had felt a moment before.

Mandy stepped forward to join the group, and the girls realized it was she they'd heard crashing through the corn behind them.

"What are y'all doin'?" Mandy asked.

They looked from Mandy to the new girl to the scarecrow. With a sigh, Cloe admitted, "We thought you were aliens."

"Aliens?" the new girl asked. "Wh-who are you? Wh-what are you doing here?"

Sasha stood up, brushing the dirt from her jeans.

"Hi, I'm Sasha," she said. "These are my friends Cloe, Yasmin and Jade, and this is Mandy —"

"My goodness!" the girl gasped, stepping forward. "You're from Bratz Magazine!" Turning to Mandy, she added, "And you're the first contestant on America Rocks Fashion!"

"Cool — you know our show!" Yasmin replied.

"I-I never miss it!" the girl said shyly, taking a step back again.

Jade glanced at the scarecrow and was surprised to see just how stylish its outfit was.

"Hey, this is the best-dressed scarecrow I've ever seen!" Jade exclaimed. "Where can I get an outfit like that? I've never seen anything like it."

"Yeah, that T-shirt rocks," Cloe agreed.

"You really think so?" the dark-haired girl asked hopefully.

"I know so!" Jade replied.

"Is that from a shop around here?" Yasmin asked. "I have to have that outfit."

"Shop?" the girl asked. "Oh, no — there's nowhere to shop around here. That's why I...I..." She trailed off, blushing and

71

staring down at the ground.

Jade looked down too and saw a cool silver design kit lying open on the ground, overflowing with gorgeous buttons, sequins and glitter.

"Wait a minute," Jade said. "You made this outfit, didn't you?"

The friends gathered around the new girl excitedly.

"That's super-stylin'!" Sasha exclaimed.

"Oh, it's really nothing," the girl said modestly. "I just put on some sequins and stuff." She patted the scarecrow on the back and added, "Skinny's my trusty model."

"How cool!" Yasmin said.

The new girl stepped forward, looking a little less shy.

"I think we should probably hit the road," Mandy announced, narrowing her eyes at the new girl. "Maybe you can tell us how to get out of this cornfield."

"Wait a sec, Mandy," Jade said. She

turned to the new girl and asked, "What's your name?"

"Sh-Sharidan," the girl whispered. "Sharidan Jones."

"Is this your corn?" Sasha asked.

"Oh, no," Sharidan replied. "I come out here cos, well, my parents think this is silly."

She gestured to the clothes with a shrug.

"What?" Cloe exclaimed. "That's nuts. You could be a real designer! Your fashions would be a massive hit!"

The friends looked at each other, their eyes lighting up with an awesome idea.

"Are you all thinking we just found our second contestant?" Jade asked.

Her best friends nodded vigorously. Sharidan's mouth dropped open in surprise, while Mandy frowned.

"Just let me run it by Byron," Sasha said, speed-dialling the show's host.

Byron answered his phone on the first ring.

"Byron here," he said. "Sasha! Where are you? You're not supposed to be using your mobile phone."

"We got lost, Byron," Sasha explained. "But listen, we've found an amazing new contestant out here and we want her to be our second pick for the show."

"Well, I don't know," Byron replied. "That's a bit unorthodox." He paused and then said, "Let me think about it. Right now, I've got to go on air. I'll catch up with you ladies later."

He hung up to begin his broadcast.

Chapter 8

"Come on – we can watch the show at my house," Sharidan offered.

The girls dashed after Sharidan and burst into her living room, where they huddled around the TV.

Byron appeared on the screen and announced, "Welcome back to America Rocks Fashion! Byron Powell here in lovely, picturesque Dayton Place." The camera pulled back to show a quaint town square with a white gazebo at its centre, then refocused on Byron's face. "But I'm here alone. Bratz Magazine took a wrong turn and Your Thing Magazine has gone completely and utterly missing. Hopefully we'll see them in New York tomorrow night in time for the show!"

At that very moment, the Tweevils were ankle-deep in muck, digging the back tyres of their truck out of the cow pond while Burdine supervised.

"It's my turn to use the shovel," Kaycee shouted, trying to grab the shovel away from her twin.

"No it isn't," Kirstee replied, yanking the shovel away.

"Yes it is," Kaycee insisted.

"Stop it, you twits!" Burdine shouted. "Keep digging!"

Back in Sharidan's living room, Cloe said, "Gosh, if we hadn't found Sharidan, Mandy would be the only contestant in the show!"

Mandy's eyes narrowed for a moment, but she covered it quickly with a pleasant smile. "Well, that wouldn't be any fun, would it?" she said, laughing.

Sharidan's mum entered the room and looked startled to see such a big crowd of teenage girls.

"Oh, honey, you didn't tell me the Girls' Service League was meeting here today," she said nervously.

"Oh—" Sharidan replied. "Sorry."

"Well, I...I guess I better bring out some snacks for all this company!" Mrs Jones said. She scurried back to the kitchen as Sharidan's dad entered the room.

"Heavens to Betsy, what a convention," Mr Jones said shyly. "C-Can I get anyone a drink?"

"I'd love one, Mr Jones," Mandy replied cheerfully. All the girls nodded in unison.

"B-back in a jiffy!" Mr Jones said.

"Why didn't you tell them about the contest?" Sasha asked, once Sharidan's dad was gone.

Sharidan looked at them apologetically and then stared down at her lap.

"Oh, girls, I'm so sorry," she murmured.

77

"But couldn't one of you take my fashions and model them for me? No one wants to see me up on a catwalk. I mean, look at me! Besides, my parents would never let me do something so crazy!"

"Oh, but Sharidan, I'm super-excited about modelling my fashions on live TV in front of the entire nation," Mandy said. "Aren't you?"

Sharidan looked at Mandy in terror.

"But they're your fashions!" Cloe protested. "You've got to model them!"

"Sounds like our girl here needs a confidence adjustment!" Sasha said.

"Makeover!" Cloe, Jade, Sasha and Yasmin cried in unison.

"Oh...I don't know," Sharidan said. But the girls had already swept her up and were rushing her out to their truck.

They parked in Sharidan's driveway and whipped out all their styling supplies. They started with Sharidan's long hair, snipping and styling it into a cute, short cut that revealed her pretty face. They brushed on eye makeup and blush, painted her fingernails and toenails, slipped cute open-toed shoes on her feet and slicked lipstick across her lips. All four girls worked together in a makeover whirlwind and when they were finished, they checked Sharidan out and cheered. She looked fabulous!

They led her outside and unfolded the catwalk from the back of their truck while Sasha pumped up some cool jams on her boom box.

"Okay, girl," Sasha said. "Let's see it."

Sharidan stepped onto the catwalk and walked slowly, cautiously down it.

"C'mon, work it, girl!" Jade called to her.

"Yeah, let's see you strut your stuff!" Sasha added. She struck a few quick poses to demonstrate, then said, "Like this."

Cloe struck a cool pose beside her. "Express yourself!" she told Sharidan.

"Chin up, shoulders back," Yasmin

instructed, walking down the catwalk with the perfect posture of a debutante.

"Get in the groove!" Sasha exclaimed.

Glowing under the girls' attention, Sharidan sped up, taking long, confident strides and even throwing in a few dramatic turns. The girls applauded wildly.

"Heavens to Betsy!" Mr Jones cried.

The girls had been so caught up in Sharidan's fashion show that they hadn't noticed her dad approaching the truck.

©MGA

"What is the meaning of this?" he exclaimed.

"Sharidan?" wailed Mrs Jones.

Sharidan stopped at the end of the catwalk, slumping back into her old shy posture when she spotted her parents. She stared at them for a moment, then burst into tears and ran back into the house.

Burdine, Royale and the Tweevils sat in the Your Thing truck, looking dishevelled and defeated.

"Where's that girl with her mobile phone?" Burdine asked.

"Good riddance," Kaycee declared. "Who needs her?"

"You can use us as contestants," Kirstee suggested.

"You don't have anyone else," Kaycee pointed out.

"And besides, we're cute and sassy on a catwalk," Kirstee finished, striking a pose.

"There is absolutely nothing cute or sassy about you two dopey girls," Burdine growled.

"Aw, c'mon," Kaycee protested. "We changed your tyre."

Royale interrupted them with a frightened whimper. The Tweevils watched through the windscreen as a cow levitated straight up into the sky.

"Wow," Kaycee whispered. "The cows here can fly."

Suddenly, the whole truck began to shake.

"What in the name of pink…?" Burdine demanded.

A bright light suddenly illuminated the entire field around the truck. Burdine looked out of the window in time to see a couple more cows get sucked up into the sky.

"Huh?" she asked.

The truck shook again and Burdine and the Tweevils heard the screeching sound of ripping metal.

Burdine freaked out and shoved her door open. She fell to the ground and started digging desperately at the mud around their rear tyres with her bare hands. The Tweevils leaned out to watch her.

"Hey, like, we already tried that," Kaycee said.

"Yeah — we, like, need a tow truck or the Jaws of Life or whatever," Kirstee added.

Burdine stood, shoved the girls aside and got back in the truck. She settled into the driver's seat and turned the key in the ignition, pressing hard on the accelerator. The truck lurched violently forward and hurtled across the field, scattering cows in front of it.

Burdine steered the truck back onto the highway and drove madly down the road, but the bright lights in the sky continued to follow her.

"It's after us!!" she wailed.

"Maybe it's the cops," Kaycee suggested. "Step on it, Birdface!"

"Ooh, yeah, it's like a high-speed chase!" Kirstee added.

"We'll be on TV!" Kaycee squealed.

The weird lights hovered in the sky above the truck, then swept to the front. Royale whimpered as Burdine slowed to a stop. A huge UFO appeared in front of the truck and landed in the middle of the highway. A massive door on the spaceship swung open and tons of little green aliens poured out, heading straight for the truck.

"Ewww! Spacemen!" Kirstee cried.

"Are we, like, going to be abducted?" Kaycee asked.

"Lock the doors," Kirstee ordered her sister.

"Maybe it's for the best," Burdine said.

She slowly leaned over and opened her door, staring at the lights as though in a trance.

Chapter 9

At the Jones' house, Sharidan sat on the sofa with her new friends on either side of her, facing her parents.

"But dear, do you really want to go to New York City?" her dad asked. "Heavens to Betsy — sounds perfectly terrifying to me."

"Your father and I just don't want you to race off with big dreams and end up with a flat tyre," Mrs Jones explained.

"But Mrs Jones, even if she doesn't win, just think how exciting it'll be," Sasha interrupted.

"Excitement can be overrated," Mr Jones replied.

"But Dad, I really want to go," Sharidan protested. "Who cares if I win? At least I tried."

Mrs Jones frowned. "Well…"

"Mrs Jones, I didn't even want to come on

this road trip — but I wouldn't have missed it for the world," Cloe said. "I mean, if we hadn't made a wrong turn, we never would have met Sharidan!"

"And we're really glad we met you, Sharidan," Yasmin added. "You rock!"

Mandy looked furious as Jade continued, "Mrs Jones, your daughter's fashions are really cutting-edge."

"Well, we'll talk it over, dear," Mrs Jones told her daughter.

"Yes," Mr Jones agreed. "We'll let you know tomorrow. But for now, you girls had better get to bed."

The four friends and Mandy staked out sofas and spread out sleeping bags, and were soon fast asleep. But Sharidan stayed up all night, working furiously away on her sewing machine. By the time the girls awoke the next morning, Sharidan had created a whole new line of clothes!

"Where'd you get all those clothes?" Jade asked sleepily.

"I made them last night!" Sharidan exclaimed, gesturing proudly to the rack full of stylish outfits. "What do you think?"

She held up an embellished pair of jeans and a sparkly tank top.

"Wow," Sasha said. "Totally glam!"

Mandy got up from the sofa and inspected Sharidan's new clothing line. She seemed to really like the outfits, but all she said was, "Not bad."

"But Sharidan, I have to say, I kind of like your other fashions," Cloe interjected. "Like the outfit Skinny was wearing when we met you."

"Yeah, they were so unique and totally innovative," Jade agreed.

"But these are more professional looking," Sharidan replied. "More, I don't know, like a real fashion designer's."

"But you are a real fashion designer," Sasha insisted.

"No, not really," Sharidan protested. "Not yet!"

"Well, it's your decision what you want to model," Sasha said. "I mean, if your parents decide to let you go."

"But we should hit the road!" Mandy cried. "We've got to make it to New York by tonight!"

"Don't worry," Yasmin told her comfortingly. "We'll get you there."

They headed out to load Sharidan's fashions into their truck.

"Are ya'll sure you want to do that?" Mandy asked. "I mean, her folks sure haven't said she could go yet."

"Try to think positively, Mandy," Yasmin replied. "They have to let her go!"

"Well, it's just..." Mandy's voice trailed off.

"What?" Sasha asked, turning to Mandy.

Sasha's best friends all paused to listen.

"I wouldn't want her to be embarrassed, is all," Mandy said awkwardly. "I mean, she's not really model material, if you know what I mean. And I wouldn't want y'all's magazine to be made a fool of."

The girls stared at her, stunned.

"Well, each person has her own style, Mandy," Cloe said finally.

"It doesn't have to appeal to everyone," Sasha agreed.

"That's what fashion is all about — taking risks and expressing yourself," Jade added. "No matter what anyone else thinks."

Mandy looked annoyed and headed back into the house without another word.

"What's with her?" Yasmin wondered.

"Yeah, for a girl who never says anything bad about people—" Sasha began.

"She sure had a lot to say," Cloe finished.

"Sharidan," Mrs Jones called from the front porch. "Can you come in here?"

Sharidan trooped inside with the others

following behind her. Mrs Jones pulled Sharidan aside and whispered something in her ear.

"Oh, thank you, thank you, Mum! Thank you, Dad!" Sharidan squealed, jumping up and down and giving each parent a big hug. "I'm so excited!"

The four best friends watched happily, but Mandy looked annoyed. She silently slipped out of the room while the others collected their things.

"Oh, heavens to Betsy, heavens to Betsy," Mr Jones said, wringing his hands. "You'll be careful on the road with my baby, won't you girls?"

"Of course, Mr Jones," Cloe promised. "But I've been meaning to ask you — who's Betsy?"

Suddenly they all heard the sound of tyres screeching outside.

"What was that?" Jade asked.

They all rushed outside, making it to the driveway just in time to see the truck peeling down the road.

"Was that Mandy?" Cloe asked.

"My fashions are in there!" Sharidan cried.

But the truck was long gone. The girls gathered in the Jones family's living room, feeling defeated.

"It was her all along!" Cloe exclaimed.

"She must have framed poor Tiffany," Yasmin said. "I can't believe we all thought she was a thief."

"A conditioner thief," Cloe added.

"She probably put the nail in Burdine's tyre, too," Jade pointed out.

"What a ruthless cut-throat!" Sharidan cried, clearly shocked.

"I mean, it's nice to have ambition, but that's just out of hand."

"I'll say," Cloe agreed.

"Well, heavens to Betsy," Mr Jones sighed.

91

©MGA

"This is just the sort of ugliness we've been trying to keep you from, Sharidan. You get big expectations, then everyone and everything lets you down."

Mrs Jones stared at her husband. "Yes, but…" she said.

"What is it, hon?" Mr Jones asked.

"Oh, nothing, nothing," Mrs Jones replied. She headed to the kitchen and then slipped out to the garage.

The girls were still sitting around and moping when they heard a cheerful car horn honking in the driveway.

"Heavens to Betsy!" Mr Jones exclaimed. "It couldn't be!"

They all looked at Mr Jones questioningly.

"What is it, Dad?" Sharidan asked.

Without a word, he stood and headed outside. The girls glanced at each other and then followed him, wondering what could be going on.

Chapter 10

The girls and Mr Jones watched from the driveway as Mrs Jones pulled out of the garage, looking jaunty in a gorgeous Classic Cruiser. Leaving the engine running, she climbed out of the car and left the driver's door open.

"Mum!" Sharidan cried.

"Honey, it's all yours," Mrs Jones said with a smile.

"Dear! Your car! It – it runs," Mr Jones exclaimed, stunned.

"It always has," Mrs Jones replied.

"Where did you get it, Mum?" Sharidan asked, as her new friends admired the beautiful car.

Mrs Jones patted the car's hood and explained, "I've had Betty here for years. I was an excellent mechanic in my day and I loved a good road rally, but I was too afraid of the risks. And you see, now I miss that feeling of not knowing what's around the next corner." She rested her hands on Sharidan's shoulders and told her daughter, "There might be disappointments, honey, but there's no sense in pulling the car over before you even get started."

Sharidan threw her arms around her mum. "Thanks, Mum!" she squealed.

"Don't forget this, honey," Mr Jones said, handing his daughter her design kit.

"Thanks, Dad!" Sharidan replied, giving him a quick hug too.

The girls hopped in the car and Sharidan pulled out of the driveway as they all waved goodbye to Mr and Mrs Jones.

Sharidan drove down the highway at a slow, sensible pace.

"So, what's the plan?" Sasha asked.

"We're going to get Sharidan's fashions back from Mandy and tell Byron she's a car thief and saboteur," Cloe declared.

"What if we don't make it in time? " Jade asked.

"Sharidan, you've got to go a little faster!" Sasha urged.

"I'm almost doing the speed limit," Sharidan objected.

But Cloe had other things on her mind.

"Oh! Heavens to Betsy!" she cried, staring out her window in fear.

"What is it?" Yasmin asked.

"Look!" Cloe cried. "It's him!"

The girls turned to look and saw the hitchhiker standing in the distance.

"It's Foul-mouthed Foley!" Sasha exclaimed.

"Dot was right!" Cloe moaned. "He's going to haunt us forever. We'll never escape him.

We'll never get away."

"Keep driving, Sharidan," Jade ordered their new friend. "Don't even look at him, Angel!"

"No," Cloe said firmly. "You can't run from a ghost. He'll never leave me alone if I don't face him now. He'll haunt my nightmares. He'll follow me all my life!" She turned to Sharidan and shouted, "Stop the car!"

Sharidan obediently pulled over to the side of the road.

"Wha-what are you doing?" Yasmin asked anxiously.

"I'm tired of being afraid!" Cloe announced dramatically, climbing out of the car. "I'm not letting him destroy me!"

Sasha turned to Jade and Yasmin and said, "She's totally lost her mind."

"Cloe, wait!" Jade yelled.

But Cloe continued walking towards the hitchhiker, whose eyes began darting around nervously as she approached.

96

"You there!" Cloe said. "Foul-mouthed Foley! I want to talk to you."

The hitchhiker took a step away from her, then another. The others hopped out of the car and ran after Cloe.

"But he can't talk!" Yasmin reminded her friend. "He doesn't have a mouth!"

"Stop!" Sasha cried. "Get back in the car. Come on!"

Cloe had almost reached Foul-mouthed Foley when he turned and ran away. Cloe chased after him, shouting, "You come back here!"

"C'mon, ladies! Let's get him!" Sasha yelled.

Foul-mouthed Foley's hat blew off as he ran. Soon Cloe caught up with the hitchhiker and launched herself at him, grabbing him around the legs. They both landed hard in the dirt.

"Ugghh," the hitchhiker grunted.

"Hold him down!" Cloe exclaimed as her friends gathered around.

The girls tackled the hitchhiker, pinning him to the ground.

"Just don't take off his scarf!" Yasmin pleaded. "Too gross!"

"Blast!" the hitchhiker cried. "Get off me, you lunatic girls!"

"He speaks," Jade said.

"He sounds familiar…" Cloe added.

She ripped off the bandana while Yasmin looked away. But when her friends didn't scream in horror, Yasmin looked up too.

"Byron!" they shouted.

"Byron Powell?" Sharidan asked, walking up to join the girls. "But you're supposed to be the show's host. What are you doing out here?"

At a signal from Byron, the camera crew sheepishly emerged from behind a hedge.

"That was stellar, Mr Powell!" exclaimed the cameraman.

"Are you all right?" the assistant director

asked. "She took you down like a rugby player!"

"I'm fine, I'm fine," Byron insisted.

"Byron, what is going on?" Sasha demanded.

"It's for the season finale tonight," Byron said calmly. "I needed something to make the show more exciting, so..."

"Yes?" Jade asked.

"So I've been filming your exciting encounters on the road with ghosts, aliens and hitchhikers – all of America's urban legends!" Byron explained.

"Gosh. That's, like, really low, Mr Powell," Sharidan said.

"You used us!" Yasmin cried.

"So the ghost town..." Jade began.

"Yes. I was Dot," Byron admitted.

"And I thought she just had a facial hair problem!" Sasha said.

"Oh! The betrayal!" Cloe wailed dramatically. "How could you do this to us, after everything we've been through together?"

"We trusted you!" Yasmin added.

"You were my role model!" Sasha exclaimed.

"I thought we were friends!" Jade finished.

"Ladies, ladies, calm down," Byron told them. "This is some of the best reality footage man will ever see!"

"You can't air any of that footage," Cloe interrupted. "I'll look like a total moron!"

"Mr Powell, we've got to leave for New York City," the assistant director announced.

"I'll see you at the show, ladies!" Byron called. "Cheerio!"

"But — Byron!" Yasmin shouted.

The helicopter landed in the middle of the highway, the wind from its powerful blades driving the girls back. Byron and his crew hopped on board and took off, while Byron waved goodbye. The girls stared after him, stunned.

"How could Byron treat us like that?"

Sasha demanded. "Forget it. He's off my hero list."

"Does this mean you guys are giving up?" Sharidan asked.

"What? No way," Jade replied. "C'mon. We've got a show to get to."

"But this time, Cloe's driving," Sasha added.

Chapter 11

A cab screeched up to a cool mansion in Manhattan, with Kirstee at the wheel. Burdine flung the passenger door open and leapt out, practically knocking over the valet.

"They almost had me. I barely got away," Burdine screeched in the valet's face, grabbing him by his jacket. "But they're coming! We're doomed!"

She released the frightened valet and charged up to the entrance of the Fashion Mansion.

"Hey, Loser Boy, what are you waiting for?" Kaycee asked from inside the cab. "We're, like, supermodels. Open our door."

The valet opened the door while the Tweevils and Royale got out.

"Now bring our bags! Chop chop!" Kirstee commanded.

They sauntered up the stairs.

"Yuck," the valet said, watching them go. "Now I see what that lady was so afraid of."

Meanwhile, the Classic Cruiser was just roaring into Manhattan.

"Drive, Cloe, drive!" Yasmin cried frantically. "The show starts in five minutes!"

"I can't believe we're in New York!" Sharidan exclaimed, peering out of the window at all the tall buildings and bright lights. "This is so exciting!"

Over at the Fashion Mansion, Byron had just started his live broadcast.

"And now, the highlight of our show – the America Rocks Teen Fashion Designer contest," he announced from the end of a totally glam catwalk. "Our first contestants, representing Your Thing Magazine, are ready to make a splash in the fashion world. Please welcome...Kirstee and Kaycee."

Kirstee and Kaycee strutted ridiculously

down the catwalk in matching pink dresses. At the end of the catwalk, they bumped their bottoms together and then held their arms in the air in triumph. The audience stared at them, unimpressed.

Backstage, Burdine was shaking Byron.

"But the world is watching! You've got to warn them!" she insisted. "The aliens are coming!"

"Miss Maxwell, you're mad!" Byron said, trying to shush her. "I am the alien leader!"

"You! I knew it! It makes sense," Burdine cried, backing away in horror. "I always knew there was something inhuman about you!"

"You see, it was all a prank," Byron explained, approaching Burdine.

But Burdine was too terrified to listen, and kept backing away until she burst onto the stage. Seeing the audience, she shouted, "It's him! He's the alien leader! Everybody run!"

The audience laughed. Burdine whirled to face them and slipped, falling on her rear and sliding down the catwalk until she crashed into her interns. The Tweevils were knocked offstage.

Two attendants in white coats grabbed Burdine and led her, kicking and screaming, out of the Fashion Mansion. Just then, the Classic Cruiser pulled up at the ultra-cool pad, and Cloe handed the keys to the valet. The girls got out of the car and watched Burdine go.

"What's with her?" Yasmin asked.

"It's only a matter of time," Burdine babbled. "They're taking over! There's no escape. Call the President. The Army. They are everywhere, you can't tell who's who!"

The girls ran up the red-carpeted stairs, only to be stopped by a bouncer.

"Sorry, ladies," he said. "The show has already started."

"But we're in that show!" Yasmin protested.

"We're from Bratz Magazine," Sasha explained.

"Bratz Magazine is already here," the bouncer said.

Burdine broke away from the attendants, shouting, "Run for your lives! The aliens are here!"

The attendants chased her and the bouncer hurried over to help them catch her. While he was distracted, the girls sneaked in through the front door. Inside a huge, super-contemporary ballroom, they pushed through the audience. Reporters, photographers, TV cameramen, supermodels, fashion designers and New York hipsters crowded around the huge catwalk that stretched across the room.

"And now, let's bring out the third contestant in our teen fashion designer competition!" Byron shouted from the catwalk.

"How did Burdine find three contestants?" Jade asked.

"Representing Bratz Magazine..." Byron continued.

Cloe, Jade, Sasha and Yasmin looked at each other, stunned.

"Huh?" they asked.

"…all the way from Rockwater Springs, it's my pleasure to introduce the lovely, delightful and talented Mandy Pickett!"

The girls and Sharidan all gasped as Mandy sauntered out, hitting the catwalk with all the haughtiness of a top supermodel.

"That's my dress!" Sharidan cried. Mandy was wearing the glitzy gown from Sharidan's sewing all-nighter.

While the crowd cheered wildly, Sasha exclaimed, "That witch!"

"What a back-stabber!" Jade added.

"What am I going to do?" Sharidan asked. "She's already modelling my fashions."

"We'll turn her in," Cloe swore.

"But what will I wear?" Sharidan cried. She shook her head hopelessly. "I can't do it. It's too late."

Yasmin grabbed Sharidan's hand and pulled her backstage.

"C'mon," she said.

The five girls pushed through the throng to reach Byron.

"Ladies!" Byron greeted them. "I was worried you wouldn't make it. Smart of you to send your girl ahead."

"Byron, Mandy stole our truck and Sharidan's fashions," Cloe explained. "You've got to disqualify her."

"Disqualify her?" Byron asked. "But she's your only contestant."

"Mandy is not our contestant," Jade told him. "Sharidan is our contestant, and Mandy is wearing Sharidan's designs."

"Who is Sharidan?" Byron inquired.

"I'm Sharidan," Sharidan replied.

"Her?" Byron asked.

"She's our contestant from Plainsville," Yasmin explained.

"But Plainsville wasn't one of the official towns," Byron protested. "You know the rules."

"Oh, you want to talk about rules?" Cloe demanded. "What about Foul-mouthed Foley? Is he in the rule book?"

"Well, you've got a point," Byron admitted. "All right, go ahead and enter her. The show starts up again in twenty minutes. Break a leg, ladies."

Byron hurried back onstage, where he exclaimed, "Ladies and gentleman, Mandy Pickett! Let's hear it for an up-and-coming fashion sensation!"

The audience clapped loudly as Mandy left the stage and came face-to-face with the girls.

"Up next, we'll introduce our final contestant from Bratz Magazine," Byron announced. "I absolutely, positively can't wait!"

"How quaint," Mandy said, glowering at Sharidan. "Little Miss Small Town comes to the big city."

"Isn't that your story too?" Yasmin asked.

"I'm better than that," Mandy snapped.

"If you're so much better, why did you need to steal my fashions?" Sharidan demanded.

"I can appreciate a little talent when I see it, but I knew those clothes would go to waste on someone like you," Mandy explained. "You don't have what it takes to pull it off. You know...that certain something special that makes you..."

"Different?" Sasha asked, raising her eyebrows at Mandy.

"You are so going down, Mandy," Jade said. "Byron's going to disqualify you."

"Who cares?" Mandy replied. "I've already got contracts lined up with two top fashion houses I met in the audience. My career is officially launched. Now, sorry, but I need to get back and...mingle."

With that, Mandy sauntered off. Cloe looked ready to tackle the girl, but her friends restrained her.

"It's not worth it," Sasha told her. "We only have twenty minutes to design a new line of clothes."

"What?" Sharidan cried. "I can't design something in twenty minutes."

"What's wrong with what you're wearing?" Sasha asked.

"Yeah," Cloe agreed. "That's the outfit we fell in love with when we first met you."

"But..." Sharidan's voice trailed off.

"It's so much more unique and original than what Mandy stole," Jade insisted. "It's you, Sharidan. That's what you need to show the world."

"Can't you take our clothes and do the same thing with them?" Yasmin suggested. "You've got your design kit, right?"

When Sharidan nodded timidly, Sasha said, "Ladies, let's get to work. It's design time!"

Chapter 12

With the help of her new friends, Sharidan embellished a whole line of clothes, adding glitter to a hip pair of jeans, painting a sassy swirl on a cute little skirt and adding sequins to a T-shirt with her trusty sequin gun. Before they knew it, the break was over and Byron was on camera again.

"Byron Powell with America Rocks Fashion," he said. "Everyone's saying Mandy's designs fit right in, but will she win the prize and walk away in the diamond go-go boots? First she'll have to beat our next contestant, a surprise entry from Plainsville."

Sharidan sat backstage, listening to the intro with her friends huddled around her. "Girls, I don't think I can do it," she said. "Maybe Mandy is right. Maybe I don't have that special something."

"Everyone has that special something,"

Yasmin insisted. "It's just a matter of bringing it out. And look at you – you're totally stylin'!"

Cloe fastened a necklace around Sharidan's neck.

"This is for you, Sharidan – for good luck."

"Oh!" Sharidan said, "thank you!"

She looked at herself in the mirror and gave her reflection a smile. She looked terrific, and she knew it!

Onstage, Byron declared, "Now let's welcome...Sharidan Jones!"

"Just get out there and express yourself, girl!" Sasha exclaimed.

Sharidan jumped up and the girls led her towards the stage. She stepped onto the catwalk, hesitant at first, but gaining confidence as she noticed that everyone was oohing and aahing at her outfit. By the time she reached the end of the catwalk, she was totally groovin' to the music.

"She's doing great," Cloe said, watching from backstage. "Let's go!"

113

All four girls strutted out in Sharidan's designs as the audience cheered. On TV, Byron tracked the call-in votes. Mandy was ahead, but Sharidan was gaining fast.

"It's absolutely, utterly amazing!" Byron cried. "The call-in votes for Sharidan are flooding in!"

Mandy sat in the audience, fuming.

"With just ten seconds to go!" Byron announced. "And nine, eight, seven, six..."

The votes were nearly even, and the audience watched

©MGA

the screens showing the results, entranced.

"...five, four, three, two..." Byron continued.

Sharidan held her breath and, just then, her total inched past Mandy's.

"One!" Byron shouted. "Sharidan is the winner of our teen fashion design competition. Join us at the end of our show when she'll model the diamond go-go boots — the only pair of their kind!"

Jade, Sasha, Cloe, Yasmin and Sharidan jumped up and down, squealing in excitement. They were too happy to notice a vicious-looking Mandy stalking by.

Backstage, a security guard handed the case containing the diamond go-go boots to Byron. The guard handcuffed the case to Byron's wrist and then slipped the key around Byron's neck.

"There you are, Mr Powell," the security guard said. "The diamond go-go boots are all yours."

"Brilliant," Byron replied.

But as Byron made his way towards the stage, he was hit over the head with a shoe. He collapsed, unconscious, while Mandy stood over him, wielding her shoe and looking triumphant. She yanked the key from Byron's neck and unlocked the case.

The sparkle 'n' shine from the diamond go-go boots was almost blinding. Mandy greedily snatched up the boots, discarding her own shoes and pulling on the boots instead. She stalked down the hall and ran into the Tweevils.

"Hey, Mandy — wanna hang with us supermodels?" Kaycee asked.

"Outta my way, you losers!" Mandy shouted, pushing them aside.

"Uh, we prefer 'runners up'," Kirstee called after her.

"She's just jealous cos we're supermodels and we had an alien encounter!" Kaycee told her sister.

"Yea-ah!" Kirstee agreed.

In the meantime, Byron lay on the floor,

moaning. The assistant director spotted him and ran over to help.

"What happened, Mr Powell?" he asked, shaking Byron awake. "Help! Someone! We need a doctor!"

The girls appeared and Sasha asked, "What's going on?" She looked down and cried, "Byron!"

"I'll get help," the assistant director promised.

Groggily, Byron muttered, "The boots. The boots."

Cloe, Sasha, Yasmin and Jade crouched on the floor beside him.

"Can you understand him?" Jade asked. "What's he saying?"

"The boots," Byron murmured. "The boots... she took the boots."

"Boots?" Cloe said.

"Does he mean the diamond go-go boots?" Yasmin wondered.

"Mandy!" Sasha exclaimed. The girls

started to go after their former contestant, but Byron grabbed Sasha's arm.

"Wait," he whispered. "I'm sorry...for everything. I was under pressure from the head of the network, but I was wrong. I won't use the footage. Can you forgive me?"

"Sure, Byron," Sasha agreed, patting his hand. "But right now, we've got some boots to retrieve."

Byron let go of Sasha. The girls darted outside and down the stairs, just in time to see Mandy waiting for her car at the valet stand. Just as the valet pulled the Bratz Magazine truck around, Mandy spotted the girls.

"Stop her!" Jade shouted. "She's got the diamond boots!"

The valet saw the boots and the bouncer came running. Mandy tried to wrestle the truck keys out of the valet's hands, but before she could grab them, Cloe delivered a swift kick to the girl's ankles and Mandy fell down. She scuttled backwards and then got to her feet and dashed down the street.

The girls chased after her, just as Byron and the cameraman came pounding down the stairs.

"Follow those girls!" Byron ordered his cameraman. "This will be the most exciting footage of the season!"

The friends chased Mandy through the darkened streets of Manhattan. They had almost reached her when she ducked down the stairs to a subway stop.

"She went down there!" Yasmin cried, pointing.

"Quick, before she catches the train!" Sasha added.

In the subway station, Mandy climbed over the turnstile without paying — no easy feat in her knee-high boots. Once she had cleared the turnstile, she trotted towards the tracks. The four best friends heard a train approaching and hurdled the turnstiles gracefully, with Sharidan following behind.

Mandy ran along the platform, peering over her shoulder as she went. The train stopped and Mandy hopped on. The four girls followed but, at the last second, Mandy slipped off, waving as the train carried them away.

"Happy trails, city slickers!" she called.

"It's the end of the trail for you, Mandy," Sharidan said, appearing beside Mandy. "I believe you're wearing my boots."

"You want 'em?" Mandy demanded. "Then come and get 'em!"

She leapt down onto the train tracks. Sharidan hesitated, but then jumped down too. As they neared the next station, Cloe,

Sasha, Jade and Yasmin appeared on the platform above them.

"Run, Sharidan!" Cloe cried.

"Forget about her!" Jade shouted. "There's a train coming!"

Sharidan climbed back onto the platform, but Mandy kept running.

"Oww!" Mandy yelled. "Help! My boot is stuck!"

Sharidan appeared at her side as the train approached.

"You mean, my boot is stuck," she said, yanking the boot free and whisking Mandy towards the platform.

The girls pulled them onto the platform just as the train whooshed past, and Byron's cameraman stood by, capturing the whole thing on film.

Later, back at the Fashion Mansion, the five girls lounged in the TV room, watching the show. They saw the police cart Mandy away in handcuffs, and then Byron, his head bandaged, broadcasting from the subway platform.

"An utterly, extremely thrilling ending to our America Rocks Fashion road trip," he declared. "Byron Powell here, headed for the hospital."

"Go Byron!" the girls all cheered.

Byron strolled in to join them. "Not bad, eh ladies?" he asked.

"You were great," Sasha told him.

"Well, it gets better," Byron announced. "Mucci Fiari has just asked me a favour — he wanted to know if I'd use my powers of persuasion to get you ladies to model his new winter line for a photo spread. What do you say?"

"Woooohooooo!!" all five girls shouted.

The next day, the girls went ice-skating at Rockefeller Centre, decked out in cute, totally hip winter gear as a photographer snapped their stylish poses for the photo spread.

Byron walked up, talking into his mobile phone.

"Mr Steel! That's absolutely, positively fabulous news!" he said.

He hung up and shot the girls a huge smile as they skated over to join him.

"Well, thanks to your exciting pursuit of Miss Mandy, our season finale was the most successful reality show on air! The network wants to do a whole new season!"

"That's fantastic, Byron!" Cloe exclaimed.

©MGA

Just then, the Classic Cruiser's horn beeped from the street. Sharidan dashed off the ice, pulled on her diamond boots and slid into the back. Her parents sat in the front, with Mrs Jones behind the wheel.

"Bye, Sharidan! Bye, Mr and Mrs Jones," Cloe called, blowing kisses towards the car.

"Have a fun trip!" Jade added, waving enthusiastically.

"Bye-bye girls," Mrs Jones replied, waving back. "Take care of yourselves, okay?"

"We'll see you again soon," Mr Jones added. "At Sharidan's next show!"

"Bye guys! Thanks for everything!" Sharidan shouted as the Classic Cruiser pulled away.

Nearby, Byron held a limo door open for the girls.

"So, what are we doing today, Byron?" Jade asked.

"Well, it's our last afternoon in the city, and there's only one thing we haven't done yet," he replied.

The girls looked at each other and smiled.

"Shopping!" they squealed in unison.

They hopped into the limo, ready to take the big city's shopping scene by storm!